The Snoring
Unicorn

The Snoring Unicorn

C. A. Rand

gatekeeper press™
TAMPA, FLORIDA

The Snoring Unicorn
Published by Gatekeeper Press
7853 Gunn Hwy., Suite 209
Tampa, FL 33626
www.GatekeeperPress.com
Copyright © 2023 by C.A. Rand

Library of Congress Control Number: 2023932694
ISBN (hardcover): 9781662937750
ISBN (paperback): 9781662937767
eISBN: 9781662937774

Hello!

My name is Willie Wisp.
Wisps are unique insects that live in the Enchanted
Forest, along with the rest of the forest creatures.
I'm quite shy, but very curious. I overheard the
council members talking about the problem
that plagues the forest. So I secretly decided
to tag along on their long, dangerous journey.
Keep an eye out and see if you can find me.
I am quite good at hiding.

Good Luck!

Chapter One

Far, far away...

beyond the distant horizon, there lies an Enchanted Forest of such immense beauty that nothing can compare with it. It is a land of peace and comfort for all the creatures who live there. Their days are filled with sunshine, happiness, and tranquility. They have nothing and no one to fear. Aiyana, Wizard of the North Mountain Lake, protects their forest.

On the outer boundaries of the Enchanted Forest lies the realm of a monstrous, sinister ghoul known as Gornoc. He, along with his servant trolls, reigns over the Forbidden Forest. This is a gloomy, grim, and dangerous place. The ghoul is a master of cheating and trickery. Aiyana exiled Gornoc and his trolls to the Forbidden Forest years ago due to their evil ways. He is not satisfied with his small territory and desires to control all the forests. But he and his trolls are forbidden from crossing into the Enchanted Forest because of a spell cast by the wizard.

One day, Gornoc encountered an old witch passing through his territory. Using his power of deception, he managed to obtain a spell to allow him to place a virus into the river that flows throughout the forests. He created the potion and instructed his trolls to pour it into the river at the point it left his territory and entered the Enchanted Forest. The more the creatures of the Enchanted Forest drank of this water, the sicker they would become.

"Ah ha!" He rubbed his hands together. "After all these many years, I have finally outwitted Aiyana the Wizard," he gloated to his trolls with an evil laugh. "Her subjects are too afraid and timid to cross my land to seek her help. She is bound to the mystical depths of the lake, as that is where she draws her magical powers. She will never know of their misery until it is too late! Once her cherished creatures die, the spell will be broken. She will have to give up her precious forest, as there will be no one left to rule."

The trolls danced and cheered at their ruler's cunning plan. Gornoc announced a weeklong holiday. The trolls and their families celebrated with music and dancing every night. They were confident their ruler had pulled off the perfect plan. Soon the Enchanted Forest would be theirs.

Chapter Two

While the trolls were busy celebrating, the animals of the Enchanted Forest were experiencing some strange symptoms. Nothing like this had ever happened to the forest residents before. It was quite alarming to say the least.

"Ollie, what was that ghastly noise?" honked Greta Goose. "I don't see how anyone in the forest got a wink of sleep last night. Ollie Owl, you must find the source of that noise," pleaded Greta. "Fly about and see what you can find out."

Ollie hiccupped as he hooted his reply, "I have never heard anything quite like it, an increasing, earsplitting noise that ended in a loud snort. It was most unusual indeed. I will speak with the other forest families and try to locate the source." He hiccupped and flew away.

Ollie's first stop was Tobias Toad. "Tobias, did you notice anything strange last night?"

"Why yes, there was a noise so loud it shook my lily pad. I almost fell off!" croaked Tobias. "Bellamy Bunny told me she was up all night trying to soothe her herd of restless baby bunnies. Why, I think it affected her too! She's so upset she is burping constantly. And I seem to be creating bubbles every time I croak."

"Most peculiar," hiccupped Ollie. "I will visit the fox next, as he is awake in the evening hours. Thank you, Tobias." Ollie flew off in search of Freddy Fox.

"Freddy, Freddy Fox, are you awake?" hooted Ollie with a hiccup.

"Who goes there? Is that you, Ollie?" yawned Freddy. "I was just trying to get some shut-eye. I had such an upsetting night. Did you hear that noise? It scared the life out of me. I couldn't stop shaking!"

"Yes, it seems it has bothered most everyone. Did you happen to notice where the noise was coming from?"

"I'm not sure, but I think it was near the twisted oak tree by the moss boulder. Isn't that close to Yazmin Unicorn's house?" Freddy nervously replied.

"I believe you are right," hiccupped Ollie. "Thank you. Sorry to have disturbed your sleep. I will talk with Yazmin." As Ollie flew away he thought, *Hmm, Freddy certainly seemed anxious. That's not like him at all.*

✦ Chapter Three ✦

Ollie flew across the lush green meadow and into the trees. He located the twisted oak next to the moss boulder and landed on the rock. He called out for Yazmin.

"Yazmin, Yazmin! May I please speak with you?" hiccupped and hooted Ollie. "It is a matter of great importance!"

Ollie heard the forest brush rustle, and soon the beautiful white unicorn with her silvery mane and tail appeared. He could detect the faint smell of lavender coming from her as she walked past.

"Here I am, Ollie. What is so urgent?" snorted Yazmin.

"The whole forest is upset. It seems there was something causing a great disturbance last night. Are you aware of it?"

"Why no," snorted Yazmin. "I had the best night's sleep ever. It couldn't have been that bad or I would have heard it. I am normally a very light sleeper."

Hmm, that's odd, thought Ollie. *How could she not have heard it?* "Yazmin, I think I will position myself in the twisted oak tree tonight and use this spot as my lookout. I will keep watch over the area to see if I can locate the source of the noise, if that will not bother you."

"Be my guest," Yazmin turned to continue grazing, "but I don't think you will find anything."

Chapter Four

The evening sun was finally setting on this troubling day. Ollie perched high upon a large limb in the twisted oak to begin his watch. Yazmin bid him goodnight as she wandered off toward her cave for the night. Ollie's head swiveled from side to side, looking for anything out of the ordinary. He spotted Freddy on the forest floor, hesitantly slinking his way through the trees. Ollie cocked his head sideways and thought, *Freddy still doesn't seem to be himself yet.* Just when Ollie thought he should move to a different location, it started. A soft, low, vibrating rumble gradually increased in volume until it was almost unbearable, then it stopped. Afterwards there was a sound of a woosh, like a breeze through the leaves, but there was no breeze. Then he heard it again, this time even louder. It was coming from the area of the cave. *I hope Yazmin is all right,* thought Ollie. He quickly flew off his branch and headed for the cave, landing on a stump just outside the entrance. He spotted Yazmin curled up inside the cave with her tail wrapped around her, but he saw no other creature. The loud ear-splitting noise began again. It almost knocked Ollie off the stump. To his surprise, it was Yazmin snoring!

"Yazmin! Yazmin!," he hooted into her ear. "Wake up! You're snoring."

Yazmin lifted her head. "What are you doing here, Owl?"

"You are snoring so loud you are keeping the rest of the forest awake!"

"Am I?" puzzled Yazmin. "How can that be? I never snore."

"There are a lot of strange things that have been happening recently. I think the forest council should meet to discuss this," proposed Ollie.

"Oh dear, I believe you are right. As president of the council, I shall call a meeting for tomorrow afternoon in the meadow. Can you notify the council members tomorrow morning, Ollie?"

"Yes, but for tonight, please try to sleep with your head on that log instead of curled up. It might help your breathing," suggested Ollie.

"Well, it will be most unpleasant, but I shall try."

The following morning, Ollie notified the forest council members of the afternoon meeting in the meadow. *What a night that was,* Ollie thought as he yawned. *I think I will get some sleep before the meeting.*

✧ Chapter Five ✧

The afternoon was warm and sunny as the council members gathered in the meadow. Yazmin called the meeting to order and addressed the members.

"First, I would like to apologize for keeping all of you awake at night. I was not aware of my snoring problem. But it seems I am not the only one who has come down with a disorder. Ollie Owl, will you give the council a list of the other ailments that have been reported to you?" asked Yazmin.

"Of course. Unfortunately there have been a few more cases reported since yesterday. I have become a hiccupping hooter, Tobias Toad croaks bubbles, Greta Goose toots gas clouds, Freddy Fox suffers from anxiety, Bellamy Bunny burps when she speaks, Freeda Ferret has become quite forgetful, Ping Panda is developing itchy pink spots, and Dean and Darla Deer are drooling. There are no common symptoms amongst the forest animals," reported Ollie.

"This is terrible; it is spreading. We need to notify the Hobbit Healer at once!" honked Greta.

"I agree," said Freddy. "Yazmin, who will you send?"

Ollie raised his wing. "I volunteer! I can fly there much faster than any of you can travel, plus I have the report of everyone's symptoms."

"Does everyone agree with this plan?" questioned Yazmin.

The members of the council were all in agreement. So, Ollie Owl wasted no time and flew to the northwest corner of the forest. He soon located Horus Hobbit's hillside home. Ollie stood outside the front door and hooted as loud as he could with hiccups in between. Finally the creaky wooden door opened, and Horus appeared with his long grey beard, wearing his ever-present brown pointed hat.

"Was that you hiccupping, Ollie? Come inside and let me examine you," encouraged Horus.

Chapter Six

Ollie entered the hobbit's home. "Oh, it's not just me. It seems the entire forest has been affected by some sort of illness. But what's strange is the symptoms are all different." Ollie proceeded to read the list of ailments experienced by the forest animals.

"This is peculiar. I've never come across anything like it! Hmm, let me refer to my *Hobbit Healers Handbook*." Horus paged through the thick manual, stopping and reviewing different sections of writing. As he closed the book, he looked at Ollie, shaking his head.

"I can offer some comfort therapies to help relieve the animals' suffering, but I do not have a cure. I believe this is some sort of virus that has affected your water. If these animals have been drinking from the river, have them go to the Sparkling Springs instead. This may help to ease the symptoms they are feeling. Your only hope for a cure is to travel through the Forbidden Forest to Mist Mountain where Aiyana, Wizard of the North Mountain Lake, resides. She has more wisdom than I. Only she can find a cure for your forest friends.

"I will supply you with a list of herbal treatments to help your friends in the meantime. Beware, a journey through the Forbidden Forest is not for the faint of heart. If your friends choose to take this journey, please do not forget these words. You must stay on the right path. The trolls will use tricks to confuse you. Always remember to stay on the right path. It is not the easy trail, but it is the only way to reach the wizard."

With that, Ollie thanked the hobbit and prepared to fly back to the forest with the hobbit's instructions. He would discuss the matter with Yazmin upon his return.

Chapter Seven

It was near dusk when Ollie Owl returned to the meadow where Yazmin was grazing. He informed her of his meeting with the hobbit. Upon hearing the distressing news, Yazmin requested an emergency forest council meeting and asked Ollie to notify the members to come at once.

With all the members of the council assembled in the meadow, Yazmin proceeded to relay the information Horus Hobbit had provided. She then suggested a plan of action. "As council president, I feel it is my responsibility to take this journey to Mist Mountain."

"That is very brave and noble of you, Yazmin, but I feel it is wise to send a delegation to represent the forest animals. It is much safer to travel in a group than alone," Ollie noted with concern.

"I agree," honked Greta with a gas cloud toot that followed. "I think the forest council should take on this task. We represent our fellow forest friends; they depend on us."

"Are we all in agreement?" snorted Yazmin. Everyone indicated they agreed. "Then we will depart at first light tomorrow morning from the meadow. Return to your homes and prepare for the journey."

The next morning, the rising sun cast a rosy hue across the sky as the five council members gathered in the meadow. Yazmin had a blanket on her back for Ollie and Freddy to rest on, so they could nap during the day. Greta had her little backpack filled with dried berries, and Ping had his satchel full of bamboo shoots to munch on.

"Greta, would you mind being our rear lookout? It might also be helpful to have your gas clouds act as a smoke screen that would help shield us from the trolls," suggested Yazmin.

"Well, if you think it will help, I am happy to comply," tooted Greta.

"Yeah, it's better for us to be upwind from that gassy skunk odor," whispered Freddy to Ping.

The first day's journey was uneventful, as it took them all day to travel from the meadow to the edge of the Enchanted Forest. Ollie and Freddy rode on top of Yazmin so they could take their morning rest. They set up camp at the edge of the forest. Freddy took the night watch, while Ollie flew ahead to scope out the path they would travel tomorrow.

Chapter Eight

The following day dawned crisp and clear as the sleepy travelers crossed the border and headed into the Forbidden Forest. No one but Yazmin got much sleep due to her thunderous snoring. The path was narrow, so they walked single file—Yazmin in the lead with Freddy and Ollie on her back followed by Ping and Greta. By midafternoon, they came to a fork in the trail. An old wooden marker announcing Mist Mountain pointed to the left trail, which was wide and smooth.

"Look, finally a trail marker," cried out Ping as he scratched his itchy back on a tree trunk. "That looks like a much nicer trail! Let's go!"

"Wait!" warned Ollie. "The hobbit said to stay on the right trail."

"That is the right trail. The sign says Mist Mountain. Why would we go on the wrong trail?" questioned Ping.

"I believe the hobbit meant right versus left, not right versus wrong. Remember, he said our journey would be difficult. Let me fly ahead to see where this leads." So, the owl took off to get an aerial view of the left trail. In a brief time, he returned with his report. "The left trail circles back to the border. It is one of the trolls' tricks. Horus warned us they would try to hinder our efforts. We must take the right trail. Hurry, as we are losing daylight."

The farther they traveled, the gloomier the day became. The trail turned wet and slimy. What small light existed was filtering through curling fog. Clouds of gnats floated through the air. Green slime dripped off black moss-covered tree trunks. There was a pond of scummy water filled with algae which smelled of rotting vegetation. Tall reeds of grass clung to its banks that barely hid a wooden sign which read Swamp of Doubt. The more the green slime clung to their bodies from dripping trees and puddles, the more they began to doubt that they had made the right decision.

"This can't be the way we are supposed to go," Freddy nervously uttered. "We are just going deeper and deeper into this swamp. We're going to get lost in here forever!"

"Freddy, grab ahold of my mane," requested Yazmin. "The lavender oil in my hair will soak through your paws and help to calm you."

"This place smells as bad as I do," tooted Greta. "I don't have a good feeling about this. This is going to take us right into the ghoul's trap. I just know it. We're doomed!"

"My bamboo shoots are getting slimed; I won't be able to eat them. I'll starve to death!" Ping panicked.

"Are you sure we didn't miss a sign somewhere? This looks like it is taking us way off course," hiccupped Ollie.

"I have kept a sharp eye out," snorted Yazmin. "This is the only trail there is. We are headed in the right direction; we must trust the hobbit. He said our journey would be difficult. This is but one of many challenges we will probably face. We must keep going. Have faith; in time we will come to the other side of the swamp."

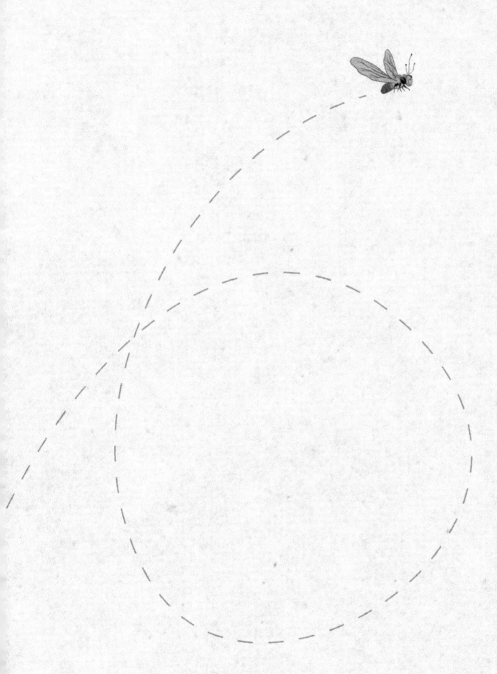

Chapter Nine

By the time the council walked out of the swamp, there was a notable change in the forest landscape. Gone was the wet, slimy trail of the swamp. Instead, the shocked animals stood looking at a bleak, barren, scorched landscape with no signs of a living thing. A sign scratched into a darkened boulder read Valley of Misery. They could feel the heat coming off the blackened surface.

"It is getting late," Owl hiccupped. "Do we camp here for the night or try to get to the other side of this valley?"

"We do not know how far this valley extends. I think it is best if we stop for the night and get some much-needed rest. Our journey tomorrow may be long and difficult. We will need our strength," recommended Yazmin.

Ollie and Greta flew back into the swamp and gathered moss for bedding. Upon their return, Yazmin laid down, stretching her neck over a charred log to minimize her snoring. They soon all snuggled together to get some rest while Ollie and Freddy kept watch.

While the council members slept, Gornoc was awaiting a progress report from his evil troll. "There you are, troll. What do you have to report?"

"I'm sorry, master," the troll quivered in fear, "but five forest members are trying to make their way to Aiyana. They disregarded our sign and made it through the Swamp of Doubt. They were last seen entering the Valley of Misery. What do we do?"

"We cannot stop their travel, but we can deter them with a few of my clever tricks," Gornoc said with a sinister laugh. "Convince them to cross the bridge of fire. The two trails run parallel for a while then separate. The left path will return the travelers back to the border from which they came. We'll have them running in circles, getting weaker by the day. It's only a matter of time."

40

Chapter Ten

Yazmin's blaring snoring woke the council members. It was the start of a new day, although you couldn't tell it. It looked the same as when they went to bed. They pulled themselves together and started walking. It was difficult to see the worn path as it blended in with the charred rocks. There was dark smoke puffing out of the mountain in the far distance. A ribbon of lava flowed down the mountain along the valley floor right next to the trail. It made the journey extremely hot and miserable. By midday, the heat was severe, and the group's energy levels were fading fast. They were hot, cranky, and running out of patience. Just ahead was a bridge crossing over the lava flow with a second path that went the same direction as they were traveling. Standing on a boulder next to the bridge, they came across a friendly-looking tiny man.

"Good day," said Yazmin.

"Greetings," replied the man. "Where do your travels take you, my friends?"

"We are traveling to Mist Mountain," stated Yazmin.

"I am going that direction but not as far as Mist Mountain. Do you mind if I travel with you? It is quite lonely traveling by oneself." The tiny man crossed the bridge and signaled them to follow.

"I see no harm in that," replied Yazmin.

"Wait, doesn't he look like a troll?" Greta whispered into Ping's ear.

"Trolls are supposed to be evil. He is friendly," whispered Ping as he munched on his bamboo.

"Then why is he so small? Doesn't it strike you funny he is the only creature we have come across since we started this journey?" whispered Greta. "Look, Owl's glasses are all fogged up. I am going to fly ahead and see where this other path leads. I'll be right back. Don't let them go anywhere before I return, Ping," warned Greta. With that, she flew off, honking and tooting.

"Where is your friend going in such a hurry?" inquired the tiny man.

"Oh, she needs to use the goose bathroom. She'll be right back. We've been walking for a long time. Let's take a break while we wait for her return," suggested Ping as he scratched his itchy pink panda pox.

Ollie Owl knew Greta was up to something. He just wished he could keep his glasses from fogging up so he could see what was going on. She suspected something; maybe this was a troll in disguise.

Yazmin and the tiny man continued to visit while they waited. Soon they heard Greta's wings flapping overhead as she approached for a landing.

"Greta, this gentleman was just telling me that the two trails run parallel, and there is a watering hole on his side of the bridge. That is where he will leave us, and we can continue on towards Mist Mountain. He said there are more bridges crossing this lava flow ahead," informed Yazmin.

"The watering hole he speaks of is a bubbling mud pot not suitable for drinking. His path will lead us back from where we came. There are no other trails heading towards Mist Mountain except the one we are currently on. It is a trick! He is a troll in disguise!" Greta angrily honked.

With that, the tiny man's disguise disappeared, and they saw him for what he really was, an evil troll.

"You are mistaken, I am sure. Why, I travel this route routinely. Trust me, I will not steer you wrong!" whined the troll as he sheepishly slinked away.

"We will not fall for your deception, troll! Be gone!" demanded Yazmin.

The troll disappeared into the black scorched rocks. Yazmin and her friends continued on the right path through the Valley of Misery. They had been walking in the extreme heat for several grueling hours when Ollie tapped Yazmin on the neck.

"Stop! I think I hear something." Ollie swiveled his neck and focused on the sound. "It sounds like rushing water. Greta, can you fly ahead and check it out?"

"Absolutely! I so hope it is water. I could use a bath." Greta flew ahead of the group to scout out the area while her fellow travelers took a rest.

Soon, Greta was honking up a storm as she returned to the group. "There's grass, trees, and a cool river! It's glorious! I know you are all tired, but we need to pick up our pace if we want to sleep in a comfortable spot tonight. Come on! It's a short distance ahead."

"Aah, cool water will feel so good on my panda pox," exclaimed Ping.

Chapter Eleven

The bunch gathered what little patience and strength they had left and forged ahead, eager to reach the forest oasis. As the trail left the Valley of Misery, the group stepped onto soft green grass and felt a cool, fresh breeze tickle their faces. It was heavenly.

The trail had turned into a soft, narrow, sandy path which led them to a raging river. As they stood aghast with puzzled faces looking across the fast-moving rapids, Freddy commented, "Um, we can't cross that!" Freddy began to panic as he nervously paced. "The water will swoop us up and carry us back to the border. Oh, this is far too dangerous, far too dangerous! Just look at the sign!"

The sign nailed to a tree read, "Beware! River of Regret. Those who attempt to cross will perish."

"I wish I never came on this journey. I'm turning pink, I itch, and now I'm going to drown! I want to go home," whimpered Ping.

"We are all too exhausted to dwell on this problem tonight. Let us find a comfortable place to sleep in this lush green forest, and we'll discuss it in the morning. Maybe an idea will come to one of us as we sleep," suggested Ollie.

So, the very tired council members laid their worries aside and got some well-earned rest. In the morning, to everyone's surprise, it was Ping who came up with a solution.

"It came to me last night as I was sleeping in the tree: tree vines!"

"Ping, what are you talking about?" snorted Yazmin.

"Vines! We cut some thick vines and tie them to the trees on this side of the river, and Ollie and Greta can fly the vines over to those trees on the other side of the river. Then they can wrap them around a sturdy limb. Freddy and I will jump on Yazmin's back; we'll all hold onto the vines as we cross the river. The water isn't deep, and the river isn't wide. It just moves fast enough to throw us off balance. If we have something to hold onto, we won't lose our balance."

"Why, Ping, that's an excellent idea. I couldn't have done better myself," hooted Ollie. "Ping, you climb up, break off several long vines, and tie them to the trees. When you are done, Greta and I will fly them across to the trees on the other side."

In a short time, the vine ropes were all attached. Greta and Ollie were waiting for their friends on the other side of the river. Ping and Freddy jumped on Yazmin's back as she hesitantly stood on the riverbank.

"Are you sure you tied those vines tight enough?" snorted Yazmin.

"Trust me, Yazmin. They are all secure," comforted Ping.

With a deep sigh, Yazmin grabbed a vine in her mouth and stepped into the rapids. She whinnied loudly as the freezing water hit her legs. Ping and Freddy grabbed their vines from atop her back. Slowly, she carefully placed one hoof in front of the other as she made her way through the icy water and slippery rocks until they were all safely on the opposite bank.

"I hope we don't have to do that again," exhaled Freddy.

"I, for one, am quite proud of us. Because we trusted each other, we were able to overcome yet another obstacle. Wonderful job, everyone!" honked Greta.

The path led them up the riverbank and into the trees. It felt so good to be in a lush green forest again. It almost felt like back home. They only had a short distance to go before they would arrive at the Forbidden Forest's boundary line. Once across, they would be in the land of the wizard. But they were so weary; the virus was draining their energy levels. It was becoming more and more difficult to continue their journey.

✦ Chapter Twelve ✦

With only a couple of miles to go, they encountered an old lady carrying a basket.

"Good day, fellow travelers." The old lady smiled. "I was just picking these ripe apples from the wizard's orchard. They are quite delicious. Would you care to have some? I have plenty to spare. They will give you the energy to complete your journey."

"Apples! I love apples!" noted Ping. "I'll take some."

"A sweet, juicy apple certainly sounds wonderful about now," drooled Yazmin.

"My lady, may I examine your apples, please?" requested Ollie.

"Why of course, you will see they are the finest apples you have ever seen," the old lady said with a grin.

Little did they know, this was the witch Gornoc tricked in order to get the virus potion. He had once again used his cunning ways to obtain her help in delaying the council from reaching the wizard in time. This was his last chance to detain them before they reached the border and entered the land of the wizard.

Upon carefully examining the basket of apples, Ollie noticed something. It was quite small and could easily be overlooked if one were not suspicious. He handed the basket back to the old lady.

"My dear lady, your apples look quite delicious indeed. Most appetizing, I must say, but we cannot accept them. You see, they have a flaw," noted Ollie.

"My apples are perfect. I assure you there are no flaws! No sweeter apple will you ever taste. Please, just try one," the old lady offered.

"Oh, but they are not perfect," sneered the owl. "Do you see that little hole next to the stem? These apples have been punctured by something. Could it possibly have been a needle with a sleeping potion?"

"Oh, that is ridiculous! It is merely a little worm hole, nothing to concern yourself about," coaxed the old lady.

"Well, if it is a worm hole, then they are not perfect apples, and we must decline your generous offer," stated Ollie smugly.

With this, the old lady grabbed her basket of apples and angrily stomped off into the forest, mumbling to herself. Once again, the ghoul's trickery had failed to hamper their progress towards Mist Mountain. But it was quite possible other factors would prevent them from attaining their goal. The travelers were bone-tired, on their last legs, and by now, quite irritable.

Chapter Thirteen

"Ping! Would you please stop that itching?" barked Freddy. "You are starting to look like a plump raspberry."

"Yeah, well you don't have to endure Yazmin snorting every five paces," grumbled Ollie. "How's an owl supposed to sleep? It's bad enough I'm jiggled back and forth, riding on her bony back!"

"Well, it's not exactly pleasant having your owl claws digging into my back every time you lose your balance, and every time Freddy has a dream, he hits me with his tail," complained Yazmin.

"You don't have the worst of it!" grumbled Ping. "Each time the wind changes direction, I have to breathe in skunk fumes from gassy Greta."

"Would you listen to yourselves?" scorned Greta. "I truly must protest. Stop your fussing and whining. Have you all forgotten the urgency of this quest? We have family and friends who are also suffering from this virus. They are depending on us to complete this journey. This is not about us; it is about helping our friends in need. We need to put aside our discomforts and stay focused on our goal."

"You are correct, Greta," said Ollie solemnly. "I fear this virus and lack of sleep has affected us both physically and mentally. We need to focus harder on the task at hand. Let us try to be more understanding of one another."

The trees of the forest were starting to thin out. They now had a clearer view of the trail ahead of them. They could see the snowcapped mountain in the distance. As they came into a clearing, there were two signs nailed to a tree trunk. One pointed to the way they had come, stating The Forbidden Forest. The other pointed straight ahead and stated Mist Mountain. They had finally made it to the border. From here on, the trail gained in elevation with switchbacks that crossed the side of the mountain. Everyone decided they would tackle the mountain climb tomorrow after they had a good night's rest. Hopefully, tomorrow would be the last day of their trek.

Everyone felt a sense of relief, as they knew there would be no more tricks from the ghoul and his trolls. As they stood looking at the trail ahead, they knew it would be a difficult climb but would yield a great reward at the end.

"This looks like a steep climb," Yazmin stated as she surveyed the trail ahead. "Grab ahold of my tail, Ping, so you won't slip and fall. Ollie, you scout ahead and let us know of any obstacles we may encounter. Freddy, you sit on my back and keep an eye out for loose rocks. Greta, keep an eye on Ping and let me know if he gets tired and needs to rest. Okay, is everyone ready? Let's start climbing!"

Chapter Fourteen

They started their journey up the mountain. At the lower elevation, beautiful green grass was spread out on either side of the path like a welcoming carpet. When they approached the first switchback, the trail became muddy and rugged. As they traveled on to the second hairpin turn, the number of rocks increased, as did the steepness of the climb. The air was cool and crisp as they continued the climb with strong determination; victory was within their sight. By now they were at a high enough elevation that fog was obscuring their view. The higher they climbed, the thicker the fog. Ollie flew back and landed on Yazmin's back with his report.

"Yazmin, the fog is too dense. I can't see the trail from up above. We will have to navigate from the ground," hiccupped Ollie.

"It looks like we are leaving the tree line. The boulders are getting larger too. That means we are very near the top of the mountain. We will stop at the next switchback to give everyone a rest," snorted Yazmin.

They took a short rest near an outcropping of boulders. There was a small waterfall trickling down the face of the mountain and creating puddles of water in the rocks. After they all quenched their thirst with the cool mountain water, the team continued on. Ping traded places with Freddy as his legs were getting tired. They cautiously walked the narrow, steep trail, paying close attention to their footing. One slip would send them all crashing down the side of the mountain. As they approached the next turn, the trail in front of them changed; it was leveling out. Through breaks in the fog, they could see the path was leading them to an alpine meadow. As they got closer, they caught glimpses of lush green grass and flowers, lots of flowers. When they arrived at the meadow, they stood in amazement. The beauty that unfolded in front of them was beyond imagination.

"So did we make it? Is this the place? Where is the lake?" Greta questioned anxiously.

"Ollie, would you fly ahead and see if you can locate the Lake of the North? We will wait for you here," snorted Yazmin.

Ollie flew in a wide semicircle and spotted a lake a short distance away. He quickly reported it back to his friends.

"I found a lake not far from here. It is at the end of this meadow, straight ahead."

As the group of travelers proceeded to walk through the meadow of wildflowers, they noticed their aches and pains were minimizing. Their mood was brightening, and their symptoms were lessening. The farther they walked, the better they began to feel. By the time they arrived at the lake, their symptoms had almost disappeared. Water lilies floated upon the tranquil, clear blue waters of the lake with snowcapped mountains in the distance. The view was breathtaking.

"It must be the cool mountain air. I feel so refreshed and energized!" whinnied Yazmin.

"I feel it too!" noted Freddy.

"Hey, my tummy stopped itching!" Ping gleefully announced as he munched on his bamboo shoot.

"It must be the altitude," hooted Ollie.

"Well, now that we have arrived at the lake, how do we call Aiyana the Wizard?" questioned Greta. "Did Horus Hobbit give you the instructions, Ollie?"

Ollie sat silently on Yazmin's back with a dumbfounded look upon his face as he adjusted his glasses.

"Ollie, Horus did give you the instructions, right?" pleaded Freddy.

"Umm, actually no. I didn't think to ask him. I was in such a hurry to deliver the travel instructions. I can't believe I forgot to ask!" hooted Ollie, looking down pitifully and shaking his head.

"What do we do now? We've come all this way and on such a long, difficult journey. Do we just sit and wait for her to appear?" fretted Freddy.

Yazmin pawed at the ground while she was thinking. "I have an idea, but I am not sure if it will work," suggested Yazmin. "A unicorn's horn has mystical powers. Maybe I can use mine to summon the wizard."

"Give it a try, Yazmin! We have nothing to lose," Greta eagerly responded.

"Okay, I'll try." Yazmin walked to the bank of the lake, bent her head down, and touched the water with her shimmering silver unicorn horn. They could all feel the ground vibrate as ripples rolled across the lake. Soon a halo of little bubbles began to rise from the center of the lake. The bubbles multiplied and got larger and larger. It was almost like a geyser was going to erupt. Then a gleaming silver sword with a sapphire-bejeweled handle jutted out of the water followed by an emerging woman dressed in a white gown with a silver crown upon her head. It was Aiyana the Wizard. Yazmin's plan had worked!

Chapter Fifteen

"Who calls upon the Wizard of the Lake?" asked Aiyana as she stood in the lake and looked upon the travelers.

"It is I, Yazmin Unicorn. We seek your wisdom. The animals of the Enchanted Forest have fallen ill due to a wicked virus affecting our water supply. The Hobbit Healer is unable to find a cure, as each animal has different symptoms. He sent us to you. Can you help us?"

"I am so sad to hear that the residents of the forest have contracted this virus. How horrible for them. Yes, I can most certainly help you! I have the antidote you seek. Do not worry. Your friends and families will soon be free of their ailments. But first, I want to hear more about your journey. In order to seek my help, the trail took you through the Forbidden Forest. That is a long and challenging trip that tests your physical and mental strength. Tell me, what did each of you learn from your travels?"

Yazmin spoke first. "Originally, I wanted to take this journey alone. I felt having others travel with me would only slow me down. I was confident I could conquer any obstacle in my way. But I soon discovered that was flawed thinking. I let my pride get in the way. I am so grateful my friends came with me, for without their help and guidance, I would never have completed the trek. I learned the meaning of trust, knowing that I can count on someone to be there for me when I need them."

"An enlightened discovery," noted Aiyana. "What about you, Owl?"

"I am known for being a wise owl. Everyone back home comes to me for advice. As we began this trip, I doubted the abilities of my friends to solve problems. I thought I would have all the answers to the challenges we would face, but I was wrong. There were times during our journey that I did not have the solution to our problem. If it weren't for my friends' quick thinking, we would certainly have suffered. I learned not to be judgmental. You never know what wisdom you will find in a friend."

"Very wise thinking," observed Aiyana. "Mr. Fox, do you have something to share?"

"I am normally a very cunning and confident fox. However, this virus has made me a twitching, nervous mess. Our travel through the Forbidden Forest was so, so long. It was extremely difficult for me to have patience. I am so grateful for the lavender oil that coats Yazmin's mane. Holding onto her mane helped to calm me. I learned that, even in the most stressful times, I could find a way to have patience and control my anxiety if I just lean on a friend."

"Not to worry, Fox," consoled Aiyana. "Your stress and anxiety will soon completely vanish."

Greta waived her wing and asked, "Aiyana, my name is Greta. I have something to add, if you please."

"Please proceed, Greta."

"I have not been the most pleasant of travel companions due to my gassy nature. Not even Yazmin's mane could cover up my skunk odor. All of us had our own irritating quirks to deal with, yet we took them in stride and tried to find a way to overcome them. We made an effort to accept each other for who we were and tried our best not to judge one another due to our ailments. I learned how important it is to accept others for who they are on the inside, not judge them from the outside."

"Well said." Aiyana smiled. "Panda, did you want to add anything?"

Ping thought for a moment, scratching his head, and then asked Aiyana a question. "Yeah, how come I don't itch anymore? My pink panda pox have all but disappeared! Yazmin isn't snorting, Ollie isn't hiccupping, Freddy seems relaxed, and Greta doesn't stink. Ollie Owl said it was the altitude. Is that right?"

"That is a very wise observation but incorrect," replied Aiyana. "Did you all drink water from the mountain on your journey to the lake?"

"Why, yes," honked Greta.

Aiyana smiled. "The water that you drank was runoff from this lake. It trickles down the mountain onto the meadow below. That is why the flowers are so beautiful and abundant. This lake water has magical healing powers. By drinking it, you have been healed. It is also how I will heal the Enchanted Forest."

"But how will you get the water from here to there?" puzzled Ping.

"Watch and I will show you." Aiyana raised her sword above her head and circled it three times slowly. A multitude of large bubbles filled with lake water rose high above her head. Once there was an accumulated mass of bubbles, with the swish of her sword, they flew south across the sky, heading towards the Enchanted Forest. "Once the bubbles reach your forest, they will burst, raining down healing water onto the rivers, lakes, and forest residents. By the time you all return, they will be back to perfect health."

"So, how do we get back home? We certainly don't want to go back the way we came. I think we have all had enough of the trolls' trickery," asserted Greta.

"I suspect the trolls had something to do with the virus getting into our water," offered Yazmin.

"The ghoul uses the trolls to do his dirty work. I have no doubt he is behind this. I will cast a spell that prevents them from going anywhere near a river or stream. They will have to get their water from the mudholes throughout the Forbidden Forest. As for your journey home, it will be quite enjoyable. But you need to decide, do you want to travel together or separately?" inquired Aiyana.

"We have come through the worst of it together. Are we all in agreement to travel back together as well?" hooted Ollie.

Everyone cheerfully agreed they wanted to stay together. Aiyana graciously nodded her head and proceeded with her farewells.

"This difficult journey has taught you all many lessons. Take this knowledge back with you and teach others. Always be thankful for this cherished friendship you share, as I am grateful for the privilege of getting to know all of you. Now, let's get you ready to travel back home. Ping, will you gather some mud from the lake bank and pack it around Yazmin's horn? We don't want it popping your bubble too soon."

Chapter Sixteen

Ping followed Aiyana's instructions, after which they all gathered tightly together in a circle. Aiyana's sword rose out of the water over her head once more. She made one large circle with her sword and then pointed it at the forest council. A huge bubble encircled them. As she lifted her sword toward the sky, the bubble with everyone inside began to rise up into the air.

"Farewell, my courageous travelers. You will be back in your Enchanted Forest very soon. Safe travels, my friends." The council members waited with joyous anticipation as she pointed the sword toward the south, and the bubble began floating through the air.

The journey back home was quick and comfortable. The council members realized an even deeper appreciation for their forest after viewing it from above. They so longed to be reunited with their families and friends. Soon they saw a familiar sight ahead of them. As the bubble gently floated down to their lush green meadow, they all cheered as it landed softly on the ground with a pop. They were all safely back home, back in the exact spot where their journey began.

About the Author

C.A. Rand writes sweet, fun, adventurous children's short stories featuring diverse, unique, and endearing characters.

Her books have a dual purpose, providing the reader with a fun adventure while they discover small life lessons and morals. She believes that by sharing someone's life experiences is how we learn compassion and understanding for others. Reading is a great way for children to experience other lives through storybook characters.

Follow her on http://www.facebook.com/authorc.a.rand and http://www.instagram.com/cindyrand_ .
Her books include *The Snoring Unicorn* and *Mysteries of the Mist.*

Printed in the USA
CPSIA information can be obtained
at www.ICGtesting.com
LVHW071313031023
759989LV00008B/392